THE MAGIC CARPET SLIPPERS

Dick King-Smith

The Magic Carpet Slippers

Illustrated by Ann Kronheimer

VIKING

VIKING

Published by the Penguin Group
Penguin Books Ltd, 27 Wrights Lane, London W8 5TZ, England
Penguin Putnam Inc., 375 Hudson Street, New York, New York 10014, USA
Penguin Books Australia Ltd, Ringwood, Victoria, Australia
Penguin Books Canada Ltd, 10 Alcorn Avenue, Toronto, Ontario, Canada M4V 3B2
Penguin Books (NZ) Ltd, Private Bag 102902, NSMC, Auckland, New Zealand

On the World Wide Web at www.penguin.com

Penguin Books Ltd, Registered Offices: Harmondsworth, Middlesex, England

First published 2000
1 3 5 7 9 10 8 6 4 2

Set in Baskerville

Made and printed in England by Clays Ltd, St Ives plc

British Library Cataloguing in Publication Data
A CIP catalogue record for this book is available from the British Library

ISBN 0–670–88525–8

Chapter One

The moment he put them on, old Mr Sloggett felt that his new pair of carpet slippers were different.

They didn't look any different. They looked the same kind he always bought, soft and comfy, in a checked pattern – blue-and-white in this case – and with rubbery soles.

But the instant he slipped his feet into

them, Mr Sloggett had a strange feeling, a feeling of great power, as though there was nothing that he could not do.

Much to Mrs Sloggett's annoyance, her husband wore slippers for almost the whole of every day. He did not go to bed in them, it must be said, and he took them off to get into the bath, but otherwise he always wore slippers. He

wore them around the house, and for messing about in the garden. He wore them for walking down the road to the postbox and even into the village.

'Why can't you wear shoes like other people?' his wife said, over and over again, and over and over again Mr Sloggett replied, 'Because slippers are more comfortable.'

But carpet slippers are of course not meant for tramping about in, sometimes in the rain, and so, about every six months, Mr Sloggett's would get holes in their soles, and he would have to buy a new pair.

Luckily there was a shoeshop in the village, not a couple of hundred metres from the Sloggetts' cottage, and a very strange little shop it was. At the front of it was a bow window, inside which stood a selection of shoes and boots and sandals and trainers and slippers, and beside the bow window was a half-door, such as you might find in a horse's stable.

The upper half was usually open, and the owner of the shop mostly stood inside, resting his arms on the lower half of the door and looking out into

the village street to see the world go
by. Above the door was a notice that
said

SHOES.
A. LOT.

Over the years Percy Sloggett and
Arthur Lot had become good friends.
Not only did Mr Sloggett buy a new
pair of carpet slippers there every six
months or so, but quite often he would
potter up the street to have a natter, and
to have a look at Mr Lot's stock of
slippers.

Each time he had to replace a worn-
out pair, he liked to choose slippers of a
different colour from the old ones. They
were always checked, but sometimes
they were black-and-white, sometimes

green-and-white, or brown-and-white, or red-and-white, or blue-and-white.

'Morning, Art,' Mr Sloggett had said only a week ago, as he neared the shoeshop and saw the owner leaning on the lower half of the door and looking out.

'Morning, Perce,' said Mr Lot.

He looked down at his friend's carpet slippers, red-and-white ones as it happened.

'You after a new pair?' he said.

''Fraid so,' said Mr Sloggett.

'Come in, come in,' said Mr Lot, and he opened the lower half of the door.

Mr Sloggett sat down on the wooden chair provided for customers, and propped his walking-stick against the counter, and took off his left slipper. It had a small hole in the sole. Then he

took off the right one. It had a big hole. Then he put them on again.

'I dunno how they gets like that,' he said.

'It's wear and tear,' said Mr Lot. 'Wear and tear.'

'The missus is always on at me to get shoes, Art,' said Mr Sloggett, 'but I likes me carpet slippers.'

'So you do, Perce,' said Mr Lot. 'So you do.'

'I'll have a different colour this time, Art,' said Mr Sloggett.

'What do you fancy?'

'Blue-and-white, please. Size ten it is.'

'I knows that, Perce,' said Mr Lot. 'I knows that.'

He reached up to a shelf behind the counter and began to take down a number of cardboard boxes. He opened them one at a time.

'Got a blue-and-white in a nine,' he said, 'but no tens, I'm afraid. No tens in blue-and-white.'

'Oh dear,' said Mr Sloggett. 'I fancied blue this time. Must be going on three year since I had blue.'

'Ah, now wait a minute, Perce,' said Mr Lot, taking down one more box. 'There's this pair, I'd forgotten. But I don't really like to sell them to you.'

'Why not?'

'The price. The price.'

Mr Sloggett looked surprised. One thing you could always be sure of with Lot's footwear: everything was amazingly cheap. In town carpet slippers were £8 a pair. Here they were £3.50. It was the same with all Arthur

Lot's stock – shoes, boots, sandals, trainers, slippers – they were wonderful value.

'Three pounds fifty you usually charge me, Art,' he said.

'I know,' said Mr Lot. 'I know. That's what's worrying me. These are only two pounds fifty.'

He held up what looked to Mr Sloggett like a perfectly ordinary pair of checked blue-and-white carpet slippers.

'I don't know where they've come from,' he said. 'Don't want you wearing them out even quicker than you usually do.'

Mr Sloggett kicked off his old slippers.

'Let's try 'em,' he said, and then when he did, he immediately felt this strange powerful feeling.

He stood up.

'And only two pounds fifty?' he said.

'That's right.'

'It's a deal, Art,' he said, and he held out a hand, saying, 'Shake on it.'

As he shook his friend's hand, Mr Lot's features suddenly contorted in pain and he gave a loud cry.

'Let go of me, Perce!' he begged. 'Let go! You'll break every bone in me hand!'

'Sorry, Art,' said Mr Sloggett.

Mr Lot fell to his knees, nursing his right hand with his left.

'Oh my word!' he said. 'Oh my word! I felt like I was being crushed in a vice! I got no idea you was so terribly strong. Whatever come over you?'

Chapter Two

'It's a funny thing,' said Mr Sloggett to himself as he walked home in his brand-new blue-and-white carpet slippers, 'but I feel as fit as a flea. Seventy-five years old I may be, but I feel more like twenty-five. Dunno what I'm doing with this walking-stick. Why, I could jump clear across the road on to t'other pavement if I tried, I bet I could.'

He looked up and down to see if there was any traffic coming. There wasn't. He looked up and down again to see if there were any people about. There weren't.

He wriggled his toes inside the new slippers, and then he bent his knees and leaped, right across the ten-metre breadth of the village street, and landed on the opposite pavement, light as a feather.

Old Mr Sloggett looked down at the new carpet slippers on his feet.

'It's got to be you,' he said.

He looked up and down again and still there was no traffic and nobody about, so he took off the slippers. Holding them in one hand and his walking-stick in the other, he bent his knees and leaped back in the opposite direction. He landed in the gutter, a metre away, in his stockinged feet, feeling at least seventy-five years old and rather foolish.

'It *is* you!' he said to the slippers, as he put them on again. Once more he experienced that wonderful warm sensation of strength and energy which seemed to rush up his body, from the soles of his feet to the top of his bald head.

Mr Sloggett gave a little hop of pleasure, at least he meant it to be a little hop but actually he rose a couple of metres into the air.

'Long jump! High jump!' he said to himself. 'And I bet I could run like a stag. Why, I could win all they Gold Medals at they O-lympic Games. Whatever will the missus think?'

But as he turned in at his garden
gate, Mr Sloggett told himself that he
wouldn't tell the missus, not yet anyway.

Mrs Sloggett was hanging out
washing on the line.

'Where you bin?' she said.

'Up to Art's,' he replied.

'In your old slippers, I suppose.'

'I goes up in me old ones. I comes
back in me new ones.'

'You're the limit, you are, Percy Sloggett,' his wife said. 'Wandering round the village in carpet slippers, whatever will people think? And you're forever buying new ones.'

'These ones are different,' said Mr Sloggett. He went into the cottage, and sat down in his armchair by the fire, and took his walking stick made of stout ash in both hands.

'Shan't want you no more,' he said, and he snapped it in two as easy as winking. Then he snapped the two pieces into four, and the four in half again, and chucked the eight bits on to the fire.

He sat for a moment watching the bits of stick burn, and then he took off his new slippers again and stretched out his legs to warm the soles of his feet.

Once slipperless, he immediately felt different, not exactly tired but just a bit lazy, a bit can't-be-bothered. He felt in fact like his usual old self who often took a little nap at this time of the day, and he closed his eyes and slept.

When he woke, it was to find his wife standing beside his chair, holding the new slippers.

'Here!' he said. 'Give them here.'

Mrs Sloggett waved the slippers at him.

'Fifty year we bin married, Percy Sloggett,' she said, 'and for most of they fifty year you bin wearing carpet slippers. T'wasn't so bad afore you retired – you had to wear shoes to work – but these last ten years it's bin slippers, slippers, slippers, day in, day out, inside or outside, come wind, come weather, till I'm sick to death of the sight of the dratted things.'

Angrily she waved the new blue-and-white slippers again.

'I've a good mind,' she said, 'to chuck these on the fire.'

'No, no!' cried Mr Sloggett, struggling to his stockinged feet. 'Don't 'ee do that, our Mary Anne, not these ones!'

'What's special about these ones?' said his wife. 'You do always buy the same sort.'

She sighed.

'If I did burn 'em, you'd go back up to Arthur Lot's, I suppose, and buy another pair just the same.' And with a snort of disgust, she dropped the slippers on the floor.

Mr Sloggett picked them up.

'Oh dear,' he said to them. 'That were a narrow escape.'

He switched on the television and sat down again in his chair. It was a quiz show, where contestants have to give the correct answers to all sorts of questions. If they do, they win a prize, sometimes a very handsome prize like a brand-new car.

Mr Sloggett watched for a moment, slippers in hand.

'I didn't know that,' he said, and 'I didn't know that,' and 'Well, I never knew that.'

Absently, still watching the screen, he pulled on his slippers.

'Now then,' said the quizmaster to the last surviving contestant, 'we come to the final question. Answer it correctly and the star prize, this magnificent three-litre supercharged Mazzorelli sports car, is yours!' The camera lingered on the gleaming silver machine.

'The final question,' went on the quizmaster. 'Or, I suppose, to be fair, I should say the final six questions. You have exactly sixty seconds to tell me the names of the six wives of King Henry the Eighth in the correct order. Start the clock!'

Before the contestant could gather his wits to say anything, Mr Sloggett put his hand up as though he were a child in class answering the teacher and shouted excitedly, 'Catherine of Aragon – Anne Boleyn – Jane Seymour – Anne of Cleves – Catherine Howard – Catherine Parr!' before the clock had reached ten seconds.

He sat watching while the final contestant made a mess of this final question and had to be content with a dishwasher instead of the car, and all the time he was thinking, 'How did I do that? I do remember the old chap had six wives but I never had no idea who they were.'

Then it dawned on him that the

magic carpet slippers not only affected
his body but also his brain!

He switched off the set.

Mrs Sloggett looked round the door.

'What was you yelling about?' she
said.

'I was watching one of they quiz
programmes,' said Mr Sloggett.

'They'm easy, they are. I could win one of they, any day.'

'You!' said Mrs Sloggett scornfully. 'Every day you try to do the crossword in the newspaper and you never fill in more than a couple of clues. And it's the easy crossword too.'

When she had gone away again, Mr Sloggett fetched that day's paper and a pen. He completed the easy crossword as quickly as he could write in the answers – in about five minutes, in fact. Then he turned to the larger, more difficult crossword. He finished it in a quarter of an hour.

Then he sat back in his armchair, grinning.

'Percy Sloggett,' he said happily, 'you bain't just a pretty face.'

Chapter Three

Mr Sloggett did a good deal of thinking before he went to bed that night. Thinking was something he had not been used to doing much of, preferring to drift along down the river of life, letting the current take him where it would.

But now, with the magic carpet slippers on his feet, thought was a very different business.

I'm a very different person, that's plain, he said to himself, in body and in mind. There's no limit to what I might do with this here secret power, but one thing's sure – it must stay a secret.

So, even though his wife seldom bothered with the daily paper, he tore out the pages that carried the completed crosswords and scrumpled them up and tossed them on the fire.

Doing this reminded him of the narrow escape his slippers had had at the hands of Mrs Sloggett. Was it possible that she would do such a thing in the future if she got hold of them again? Should he keep them on in bed? Better not, she'd make an awful fuss.

In the end he delayed coming up to bed till his wife was asleep, and then he

put the slippers under his pillow. Then
he put his head on it and drifted off
into dreamland. I know that old king
had six wives, was his last thought, but I
got no idea what they was called.

When he woke next morning, Mr
Sloggett lay pretending to be still asleep,
until his wife had got up and dressed
and gone downstairs. Then he threw

back the covers and swung his legs over the side of the bed and pulled the new slippers from under the pillow. He held them a moment and tried again to remember the names of Henry VIII's wives. Not a clue. He put them on his feet and immediately the six names tripped off his tongue in the correct order.

'You'd never believe it,' he said to himself, 'and all for two pounds fifty.'

But then it suddenly struck him that the life of each pair of his slippers was always a short one: six months at most, and sometimes a good bit less.

How could he preserve these ones from wearing out? By not wearing them, of course, or only very seldom. Should he buy another pair of slippers from Art, to wear most of the time?

'No, blow that,' said Mr Sloggett. 'Let's have fun with these while they last. You never know, they might last for ages, being magic ones. Last longer than me perhaps. I bain't no spring chicken.'

At breakfast, Mrs Sloggett looked up at the calendar that hung on the wall behind her husband.

'Thirtieth of October already,' she said. 'Afore you can look round it'll be Christmas.'

Mr Sloggett did not look up from his cornflakes.

'Fifty-six days,' he said. 'Fifty-six days to Christmas.'

'You done that quick,' said Mrs Sloggett.

''Tis easy. Two more of October, thirty of November, and twenty-four out of December. Any fool could do that.'

'So it seems,' said Mrs Sloggett. 'Next thing you'll be telling me how many hours it is.'

'One thousand, three hundred and forty-four,' said Mr Sloggett. He looked at his watch.

'Minus nine,' he said, 'because it's already nine o'clock this morning. So 'tis only one thousand, three hundred and thirty-five hours to Christmas. Or eighty thousand, three hundred and forty minutes. Or four million, eight hundred and twenty thousand, four hundred seconds.'

Mrs Sloggett laughed scornfully.

'Don't be so daft, Percy,' she said. 'Making up all they figures.'

After breakfast Mr Sloggett walked

up the street to Arthur Lot's shop, and as he did so, a thought struck him.

The blue-and-white slippers on his feet were magic ones, he was in no doubt at all about that. But were they only magic for him? Would they work for someone else? For Art, for example?

Oh, I hopes not, he said to himself, but there's only one way to find out.

Arthur Lot was leaning on his half-door as usual.

'Morning, Perce,' he said. 'Come on in. How's the new slippers?'

'Brilliant,' said Mr Sloggett. 'You got any more like that, Art?'

'No,' said Mr Lot. 'Just an odd pair, they were.'

They are, thought Mr Sloggett.

'See any telly last night, Art?' he asked.

'A bit.'

'See that quiz programme?'

'I did. Shouldn't have minded winning that car, I shouldn't. Better nor our old Ford.'

'You'd have known the answer to that last question, would you? The names of Henry the Eighth's six wives?'

'Bless you, no,' said Mr Lot. 'Never got on with history at school.'

'But you must have heard the chap

read out the right names in the right order?'

'Never listened.'

'So you don't know none of 'em?'

'Haven't got no idea.'

There was a short silence, and then Mr Sloggett said, 'What size do you take, Art?'

'Same as you, Perce. Tens.'

'Like to try these slippers on?'

'Whatever for?'

'They'm ever so comfy. Best pair I've ever had. Go on, try 'em.'

'Oh, all right then,' said Mr Lot. 'If I must.' And he took off his shoes.

'Hope nobody comes in the shop,' he said. 'I shall feel daft.'

As soon as Mr Sloggett had taken off his slippers, he found, once again, that the names of the King's wives had

completely escaped from his memory.
But oh, he thought, how I hopes that
Art doesn't know them now that he's
wearing the slippers.

'Did you mean what you said, Art?'
he asked.

'When I said what?'

'That you didn't know the answers to
that question about Henry the Eighth?'

'Course I meant it.'

'And you still don't know? Now?'

'Course I don't,' said Mr Lot. 'Look,
Perce, I never even knew the old fellow
had six. One's too much for me
sometimes. Here, have your precious
slippers back.'

Chapter Four

Mr and Mrs Sloggett had never had any children.

Mr and Mrs Lot, on the other hand, not only had a son but also a granddaughter who quite often came to stay with them.

She was a happy kind of child with curly red hair whose name was really Laura, but ever since she was quite small she had always been called Lollie.

And ever since she was quite small she had known her grandfather's friend Mr Sloggett, whom she called Uncle Percy.

Percy Sloggett never said as much to anyone, not even to his wife, but he would dearly have loved a grandchild of his own, preferably a little girl, preferably a little girl with curly red hair, exactly like Lollie Lot.

Whenever she came to stay with her grandparents above the shoeshop, Mr Sloggett dropped in rather more often than usual, and the same conversation took place each time.

'Morning, Art,' Mr Sloggett would say.

'Morning, Perce.'

'And morning, Lollie.'

'Morning, Uncle Percy.'

'I don't suppose Lollie would like to come along o' me to the sweetshop next door, would she, Art?'

'I don't suppose she would, Perce.'

'I would, Grandad! I would, Uncle Percy!' Lollie would cry, and off they'd go, the tall bald old man and the small red-haired girl.

'You spoil her worse than I do, Perce,' Mr Lot would say when they returned.

'It's only just this once, Art.'

'A likely story, Perce! I say, a likely story!'

And sure enough, if Lollie stayed for a week, Uncle Percy would drop in to the shoeshop six times. He didn't come on a Sunday, of course – the shop was shut – and he never stayed too long, but

Lollie Lot's visits came to mean a great deal to him.

Not long after he had bought the magic carpet slippers, she came to stay with her grandparents. Soon, to nobody's surprise, Mr Sloggett turned up at the shoeshop.

It was while he was buying sweets for Lollie that a happy thought struck him.

Having firmly decided to keep the magic of the carpet slippers a secret from his wife, from Arthur Lot, from anyone, he now suddenly realized that in fact he did very much want to tell someone.

Who better to tell than a child? For children, very sensibly, believe in magic. What better child to tell than Lollie Lot?

So as they walked the few metres

back from sweetshop to shoeshop, Mr Sloggett stopped, and, pointing down, said, 'What have I got on my feet, Lollie?'

'Slippers, Uncle Percy,' said Lollie. 'You always wear slippers.'

'Yes, but these are different.'

'They look new.'

'So they are, but that's not what makes 'em different. Now then, can you keep a secret?'

Lollie took a bite from her chocolate bar.

'Yes,' she said.

'You must promise not to tell anyone – not your dad nor your mum nor your grandad nor your grandma nor none of your friends neither. This is just between you and me, understand?'

Lollie took another bite.

'Yes,' she said.

'Promise?'

'Yes, Uncle Percy, I promise.'

'Right then,' said Mr Sloggett, and he pointed down once again. 'These here carpet slippers,' he said, 'are magic ones. When I'm wearing them, there's nothing I don't know and nothing I can't do.'

'Show me,' said Lollie.

'All right. What d'you want me to do?'

'Fly,' said Lollie.

'Fly?'

'Yes. Fly. Like a bird.'

'Don't be silly, Lollie, I can't do that.'

'You said there was nothing you couldn't do.'

'Nothing that ordinary folk can do. But flying – why, no one can do that.'

'All right,' said Lollie. 'Well then, stand on your head. Anyone can do that.'

'Hm,' said Mr Sloggett. 'Tell the truth, I bain't too sure how to go about that.'

Lollie finished her chocolate bar.

'You kneel down,' she said, 'and you put the top of your head down on the

ground and your hands flat on the
ground either side of your head and
you kick your legs straight up in the air.'
Mr Sloggett wiggled his toes inside

his magic carpet slippers. C'mon, Percy, he said to himself, you can do it. He knelt down and put the top of his head down on to the pavement and his hands flat on either side and kicked up his legs and straightened them.

'This what you mean?' he asked, upside down.

'That's brilliant, Uncle Percy,' said Lollie. 'That's magic, that is!' and she stood on her head beside him.

At which moment Arthur Lot poked his head out over the half-door of the shoeshop, to see his granddaughter Lollie and his old friend Percy Sloggett standing on their heads on the pavement, one on her red curls, one on his bald noddle.

Chapter Five

Mr Lot came out of his shop and bent down and peered into Mr Sloggett's upside-down face.

'I never knew you could do that, Perce,' he said. 'I say, I never knew you could do that.'

No more did I, thought Mr Sloggett.

'There's always a first time,' he said.

He let his legs come down again until

he was once more standing on the pavement in his carpet slippers.

Beside him, Lollie did the same.

'Uncle Percy's clever, isn't he, Grandad?' she said.

'I should say so!' said Mr Lot. 'What else can you do, Perce?'

Anything, thought Mr Sloggett, so long as I'm wearing these here slippers. Except fly.

'Oh, I don't know,' he said.

'I'll tell you something, Lollie,' said her grandfather. 'Uncle Percy's ever so strong. Why, only the other day we shook hands and he near broke every bone in mine. You mind you don't ever go shaking hands with him.'

'I wouldn't hurt Lollie, Art, you knows that,' said Mr Sloggett.

'Well, you hurt me.'

'Didn't know my own strength,' said Mr Sloggett truthfully.

Just then a customer went into the shoeshop and Mr Lot hurried back inside.

'Was that really the first time you ever stood on your head, Uncle Percy?' said Lollie.

Mr Sloggett nodded.

'And are you really really strong too? Like Grandad said?'

Mr Sloggett nodded again.

There was a car parked beside the kerb, and he took hold of the back of it and lifted the rear wheels right up off the ground.

'Wow!' said Lollie.

'It's these here slippers that does it, like I told you,' said Mr Sloggett. 'They make me clever too. Ask me a question, Lollie, any question. I'll bet I can answer it.'

Lollie thought for a bit. Then she said, 'How high is Mount Everest?'

'Eight thousand, eight hundred and

forty-eight metres,' said Mr Sloggett. 'Or, if you prefer, twenty-nine thousand and twenty-eight feet. Ask me another.'

'What are the names of the Prince of Wales?'

'Charles Philip Arthur George.'

'Well, here's one you won't know, Uncle Percy,' said Lollie. 'What are the names of the Spice Girls?'

'Posh, Baby, Sporty, Scary. Ginger has left, of course.'

'Wow!' said Lollie.

She looked down at Mr Sloggett's slippers.

'Would they work for me if I put them on?' she asked.

'No. They only work for me.'

'You're lucky, you are,' said Lollie. 'Being so strong and so clever too. Fancy you knowing the names of the

Spice Girls. I suppose you know the names of the brothers in Oasis too?'

'Course I do,' said Mr Sloggett. 'There's Liam Gallagher and Noel Gallagher.'

Lollie shook her red curls in wonderment. 'Wow-eeee!' she cried.

Back home again, Mr Sloggett sat down in his armchair and took off his slippers to toast his toes.

In the kitchen Mrs Sloggett had the radio on, rather loud.

Some kind of music boomed out.

Mrs Sloggett came in.

'Oh, you're back,' she said.

'What?' said her husband. 'Can't hear you with that racket going on. What is it anyway? Who is it making all that row?'

'Calls theirselves Oasis,' said his wife.

'Oasis?' said Mr Sloggett. 'Never heard of 'em.'

Chapter Six

Mr and Mrs Sloggett's fifty years of married life had, though childless, been on the whole a happy time.

Not that a fly on the wall would always have thought so, for often they would snap at one another in what might have sounded quite an angry way. These little spats might be about a variety of things, the commonest being that – in Mr Sloggett's opinion – his wife always had the radio on *much* too loud (she was a trifle deaf), and – in Mrs Sloggett's view – that her husband *would* wear slippers.

But neither ever bore lasting grudges, and never had they gone to sleep at nights still on bad terms.

They did not tell each other so, but each was in fact very fond of the other.

During that November Mr Sloggett began to think hard about what to give his wife as a Christmas present. Christmas had always been very important to Mary Anne Sloggett, and her husband had always tried to choose something nice as a gift. But of course they were not well off, and the things he could afford were very modest.

Now surely, with the aid of the magic

carpet slippers, he would somehow be able to surprise her with a really special present.

So far he had used the magic quite sparingly. It was nice of course to be able always to complete the harder crossword in the newspaper (the easy one was now too simple to bother with): he did not write in the answers but solved the whole thing in his head. Likewise if there was a quiz – general knowledge or any specialist subject – on telly, he would answer all the questions correctly but never speak the answers aloud.

At times too he used the physical powers that the slippers gave him. For example, one evening after dark he was in a hurry to catch the last post, and he ran down the road to the pillar-box at a

speed that an Olympic athlete would have envied.

On another occasion, he decided to chop down an old tree in the hedge at the bottom of the cottage garden. It was quite a big tree, with a trunk as thick round as a telegraph post, but Mr Sloggett in his slippers gave one swing of his axe and sliced through it as though it had been a stick of rhubarb.

In the matter of Mrs Sloggett's Christmas present, however, it wasn't his strength he was planning to use but his brains. What should he get her? It must be something she'd always wanted but never been able to have because of the cost.

December came and Mr Sloggett had still not decided what to do, when one day Fate decreed that he should notice an advertisement in his daily paper.

He had kicked off his slippers to warm his feet, and thus become his old slow-thinking self as he read this advertisement, which was for a washing-machine.

For a while Mr Sloggett sat by the fire in a doze. Then, his feet warm, he pulled on his slippers again.

The paper on his lap was still open at the same place, but now the words of the advertisement simply leapt out of the page at him!

A washing-machine! he thought. Just what Mary Anne's always wanted! All these years she's been washing our clothes in the old copper and scrubbing

them on the old washing-board and
putting them through the old mangle
and carrying them out to the line and
pegging them up. Now, if only I could
get her this here machine for Christmas.
But how could I afford it?

He turned the page, and there, to his amazement, was the answer.

THIS WEEK'S
'DO YOU KNOW?'
COMPETITION.
HERE ARE THREE QUESTIONS.
ANSWER EACH CORRECTLY
AND YOU COULD WIN
£1,000!

A thousand pounds! thought Mr Sloggett. I could get the washing-machine and a penny change too. He read on.

1. Is Big Ben
    a)   a tower
    b)   a bell
    c)   a clock

2.   Elvis Presley's house is called
     a)   Brooklands
     b)   Shadowlands
     c)   Gracelands

3.   Which of these birds can fly
     backwards?
     a)   the secretary bird
     b)   the humming bird
     c)   the mocking bird

Easy as falling off a log, said Mr Sloggett to himself, and he wrote on the coupon

1.b   2.c   3.b

and filled in his name and address and put it in an envelope and stamped it.

'Just going up to post,' he called to his wife.

'In your carpet slippers, I suppose,' said Mrs Sloggett.

'Course.'

'Who're you writing to?'

'Doing a competition. Out of the newspaper.'

'Competition? You couldn't never win one o' they.'

'You might be surprised,' said Mr Sloggett.

'Pity you got nothing better to do,' said Mrs Sloggett. 'Me, I got a great pile of washing to get through. I wish to goodness I had one o' they washing-machines.'

'P'raps Father Christmas will bring you one,' said Mr Sloggett to himself, as he made his slippered way to the postbox.

Chapter Seven

It can only have been luck – nothing to do with the magic carpet slippers but luck, pure and simple. Quite a large number of people who entered the 'Do You Know?' competition gave the correct three answers, but Mr Sloggett's envelope was the first to be opened and thus he was adjudged the winner.

And it can only have been luck that

the makers of the new luxury Magiclean washing-machine with tumble-drier should arrange to have it delivered and installed in the week before Christmas, when Mrs Sloggett happened to be away. Her sister had been poorly and she had gone to look after her for a few days.

When she returned home, on Christmas Eve, the third stroke of luck decreed that she should have no need to go out to the wash-house at the back of the cottage that evening.

So that on the morning of Christmas Day Mr Sloggett was able to take his wife by the hand and say, 'I got something to show you, Mary Anne, so shut your eyes and don't open 'em till I says so.'

Then he led her out to the wash-house and said, 'Right. You can look now.'

Mrs Sloggett opened her eyes an ordinary amount and then she opened them very wide indeed.

'Percy!' she cried. 'Whatever . . .?'

'Happy Christmas,' said Mr Sloggett, 'and many happy wash-days.'

'However . . .?' gasped Mrs Sloggett.

'I won it,' said her husband. 'That competition I done, you said I wouldn't never win one o'they, but I did.'

'Oh Percy!' said Mrs Sloggett, and then, after she had given him a big hug, she rushed off straight away to get some dirty clothes and made him show her how to work it (which the Magiclean people had shown him). The washing-machine washed and then the tumble-drier tumbled and dried, and

altogether it was a very happy
Christmas.

For a little while after that, Mr
Sloggett didn't make much use of the
slippers' magic properties. He solved his
crossword, to be sure, and got all the
answers right in television quizzes, and
occasionally ran very fast or jumped
very high or lifted enormous heavy
weights, when no one was looking.

But though he didn't actually use the
power of the slippers for a particular
purpose, he thought very seriously
about the whole business. I could go in
for lots of competitions, he thought,
and maybe win even bigger prizes. Like
a car, say, but then that wouldn't be no
good, I can't drive so I don't want one.

Now Mary Anne, she *wanted* a
washing-machine, and now she's as

happy as a dog with two tails, but me, I'm contented as I am, there's nothing much I need. All I want is for these here carpet slippers to last for ever.

Sitting in his armchair by the fire, he took off the slippers, feeling immediately just a bit lazy, a bit can't-be-bothered, as usual, and examined them. Not surprisingly, they looked a bit worn. They *had* been worn, all the time, during the three months or so of their life so far, and the rubber soles were beginning to look a bit thin.

Slipperless, Mr Sloggett didn't really care all that much. Another three months, he thought, and they'll probably be wore out. So what? He pulled them on again.

Slippered now, experiencing the usual strange feeling of power, he answered

himself. So I'd better get a move on and
think of something to use them for. But
what?

I can't ask Mary Anne, nor Art Lot,
nor anyone – they don't know about
them. Wait a minute though! One
person does – Lollie! I'll ask her.

Mr Sloggett jumped out of his
armchair and strode purposefully out of
the room, remembering to slow down

to his usual amble as he passed through the kitchen.

'Where are you going?' said Mrs Sloggett.

'Up the village.'

'In those old slippers, I suppose.'

'Yes. Going to see Art.'

'Buy some new ones, I suppose?'

'No, no,' said Mr Sloggett. 'These have got years of wear in them yet.' Or months anyway, I hopes, he thought, as he walked with long strong strides up the road.

Arthur Lot was leaning on his half-door, looking out, as usual.

'Arternoon, Perce,' he called. 'I got a friend of yours here,' and he opened the half-door and stood aside and out came Lollie Lot.

'Hello, Uncle Percy,' she said.

'Well, well,' said Mr Sloggett. 'Fancy you being here, Lollie. There's something I want to ask you.'

'And I know what it is, Perce,' said Mr Lot. 'Would she like to go along to the sweetshop? Am I right?'

'Well, yes, you're right,' said Mr Sloggett.

'Just so happens there's something I want to ask you, Perce,' said Mr Lot. 'If you've got a bit of time to spare.'

'Long as you like, Art.'

'Well, I promised to take Lollie down to the village playground while the missus looked after the shop, but she's had to go out. So I wonder, would you like to take Lollie down there?'

'Course I will,' said Mr Sloggett.

Lollie grinned.

'After we've been to the sweetshop,

Uncle Percy?' she said.

So it came about – pure luck, nothing to do with the slippers – that Mr Sloggett had quite a nice long time alone with his red-headed young friend, as she swung on the swings and slid down the slides and bounced on the bouncy castle.

Out of breath at last, she sat on a bench beside her bald-headed old friend.

'Lollie,' said Mr Sloggett. 'You know these magic slippers of mine. I told you about them, remember?'

'Yes, Uncle Percy.'

'You haven't told nobody about them, have you?'

'No, Uncle Percy.'

'Well, since I saw you last, I used them to get all the answers right in a

competition and win it. I won a new washing-machine for Mrs Sloggett.'

'Wow!' said Lollie.

'But I don't know what to use them for next. There's nothing I particularly wants for myself and I got no children nor grandchildren. Though I'll tell you summat, Lollie. If you were my granddaughter instead of Art's, I'd use 'em to get you a really nice present. Come to think of it, why shouldn't I get you a present anyway? Would you like that?'

'I would, Uncle Percy,' said Lollie Lot.

'Is there something you'd really like?' asked Mr Sloggett. 'Anything, doesn't matter what it costs. A bike perhaps?'

'I've got one.'

'A watch?'

'I've got one,' said Lollie. 'But I'll tell you what I'd really really like to have, Uncle Percy.'

'What?'

'A pair of magic carpet slippers, like yours.'

Chapter Eight

'Oh, I don't know about that, Lollie love,' said Mr Sloggett. 'I don't know if there are any other magic ones in the world bar mine.'

'Well, could I try yours on, Uncle Percy? Just to see what happens.'

'Nothing will,' said Mr Sloggett. 'I got your grandad to wear 'em and they didn't do nothing for him. They only works for me.'

'Can't I try?'

'Oh, all right,' said Mr Sloggett. 'Take your shoes off then.' And he took off his slippers and Lollie shoved her small feet into them.

'Feel any different, do you?' asked Mr Sloggett.

'How d'you mean?'

'Well, powerful-like, as though you could answer the hardest question or jump right over my head.'

'No,' said Lollie. 'Ask me a hard question.' But of course Mr Sloggett with his slippers off couldn't think of one.

'I'll try jumping,' said Lollie, and she got off the bench and bent her knees and jumped upwards as high as she could. But it was only an ordinary sort

of a jump and all that happened was
that the slippers fell off.

Lollie shook her red head, grinning.

'You're right,' she said. 'They won't
work for me. Put them on again, Uncle
Percy, and show me what they do for
you.'

So Mr Sloggett put on his magic slippers again, feeling at once that thrill of power, and looked around the playground to see if anyone was watching.

But there was no one else about, so he sat on one of the swings and said, 'Watch this.'

Then he began to swing himself, higher and higher and higher, until the swing swung right round over the top of its frame. Lollie watched delightedly as Uncle Percy whizzed up and over and down and up and over and down, faster and faster, spinning round and round like a Catherine Wheel.

'Wow!' cried Lollie when at last the swinger came to a halt. 'That was mega, Uncle Percy! I wish Grandad and Grandma could have seen you!'

'You're not to tell them, mind,' said Mr Sloggett.

'Oh, no.'

'Right then, we'd best be getting back. And you have another think about a present, but don't tell them about that either. Whatever I do for you, it'll just be a secret between you and me. OK, Lollie?'

'OK, Uncle Percy,' said Lollie Lot as they left the village playground. Little did she dream that, not five minutes later, her friend would, thanks to the power of his magic carpet slippers, give her the greatest present of all – her life.

It happened after they had rounded a corner in the village street and had come to a spot directly opposite that old familiar shop above whose door was a notice that said

SHOES.
A. LOT.

'Hold my hand while we cross the road,' said Mr Sloggett to Lollie, but at that moment, before she could obey, Arthur Lot looked out and waved and called, 'Hullo, Lollie!'

'Hullo, Grandad!' cried Lollie, and without thinking, without looking to left

or to right, she ran across the road towards her grandfather.

At that precise instant a car swung round the corner, a car that was travelling much too fast, a car that had no hope, it seemed, of missing the small red-headed girl in the middle of the road.

Afterwards, Mr Lot could never really recall what happened.

He remembered shouting, 'Look out!'

He remembered the squealing of brakes, he remembered the sight of the car swerving and skidding and the dull sound of an impact.

And he remembered especially the overwhelming sense of relief as his granddaughter stumbled and tumbled on to the pavement right in front of the shoeshop and got to her feet and rushed into his arms, unhurt.

But the man who had saved her life, the man who, with one incredible lightning leap – which Mr Lot did not see but which must have measured the best part of ten metres – had pushed her out of the way of the car, was hurt.

For there in the road lay the tall bald-headed carpet-slippered figure of Percy Sloggett.

Chapter Nine

After the ambulance had come and gone, the police who were questioning the car driver were puzzled by his version of what had happened. In his shock he had freely admitted that he'd been driving much too fast, that it was all his fault, that he deserved whatever punishment he should get.

But he also swore blind that the man

who had been hurt had saved the child by an enormous leap such as no ordinary human being could possibly make.

'Let alone an old chap like him,' said the driver. 'I never saw anything like it. Talk about the world long jump record, why, he'd have smashed that easy. I tell you, he flew through the air like a bird.'

After that, they breathalysed the man of course, confident that he must be well over the limit, but he was quite sober.

As for Mr Sloggett, he was reasonably lucky – ordinary luck, nothing to do with the slippers – in that, instead of being killed, he simply broke both legs.

'Nice clean breaks,' said the surgeon cheerfully to Mrs Sloggett when her husband had come round from the

operation. 'We'll soon have him on his feet again.'

'In your slippers as usual, I suppose,' said Mrs Sloggett when the surgeon had gone. 'What in the world were you up to, Percy, anyway? Chap of your age trying to play the hero. Who d'you think you are, Superman?'

'She's all right, is she, Mary Anne?' said her husband. 'Lollie Lot, I mean.'

'Silly child,' said Mrs Sloggett. 'Running over the road like that without looking. They told me, the Lots did. They're ever so grateful to you, they are, not surprising. They'll be coming in to see you, soon as they're let. Now, you get some sleep, Percy. I'm taking all your clothes back home to put in my washing-machine.'

'Not my slippers,' said Mr Sloggett.
'Don't take them.'

'You and your precious slippers,'
said Mrs Sloggett. 'What good are they
to you when both your feet are in
plaster?' but all the same she left them
behind.

Next morning the Lots and Lollie
came into hospital to visit.

The grandparents could not thank
Mr Sloggett enough.

'If it hadn't been for you . . .' said
Mrs Lot and then stopped, unable to
continue.

'It was all my fault, Uncle Percy,' said
Lollie. 'If I hadn't run across the road
like that . . .'

'Don't you fret, Lollie,' said Mr
Sloggett. 'My legs will soon mend, and
then the next time you come to stay with

your grandad and grandma, perhaps
we'll go down to the playground again.'

Lollie grinned.

'And have a swing?' she said.

'I just don't know how you were
quick enough to shove her out of the
way, Perce,' said Mr Lot. 'You must

have moved like greased lightning.'

He looked at the pair of size ten checked blue-and-white carpet slippers that stood on top of Mr Sloggett's bedside cupboard.

'And wearing them things too,' he said, 'as per usual.'

Mr Sloggett caught Lollie's eye and winked.

'Can't wear them at present,' he said, pointing at his plastered feet.

'Tell you one thing, Perce,' said Arthur Lot. 'You're never going to have to pay for another pair of carpet slippers in my shop. You'll get them for nothing, for the rest of your natural.'

'Perhaps these ones will last Uncle Percy for ever, Grandad,' Lollie said.

Her grandfather picked the slippers off the cupboard and inspected them.

Mr Sloggett's landing at speed from
that life-saving leap had done the soles
no good at all.

'They're fair wore out,' said Mr Lot.

After the Lots had gone, Percy
Sloggett lay trying to recall that feeling,
of power of mind and power of body,
which surged through him each time he

put on his magic carpet slippers, but he could not recapture it.

Doesn't matter, he thought to himself in that lazy can't-be-bothered way. I might be better off without them. All they've brought me is two broken legs. Who knows, next time I might break my neck.

He took the slippers off the cupboard and held them up before his face, one in each hand. Scuffed and threadbare and dirty they were from the everyday use they'd had, and, turning them over, he saw that each had more holes than sole.

'Art's right,' he said to them softly. 'Your life is over. But what you'll never know is that you saved a life. Not me, t'wasn't me, t'was you as saved the life of little Lollie Lot.'

When his wife was leaving after visiting him that evening, he said to her, 'Take these slippers with you, Mary Anne, and chuck them on the fire.'

'On the fire?' said Mrs Sloggett. 'Why, you made an awful fuss once when I said I was going to do that. You feeling all right, Percy?'

'Yes,' said Mr Sloggett. 'I'm all right.
And by the way, Art says I needn't
never pay for carpet slippers from now
on, so you might go up to the shop and
choose me a new pair, ready for when I
gets all this plaster off. I think I fancy

green-and-white check ones this time.'

Mrs Sloggett sighed, shaking her head. I don't know, she thought. Him and his carpet slippers. They're all the same, anyway.

'I'll go and ask the nurse for a carrier-bag to put them in,' she said. 'Don't want to be seen carrying such scruffy old things.'

When she had gone, Mr Sloggett put a hand inside each slipper and gently patted the worn soles together in a clapping motion.

'Well done,' he said. 'I shan't forget you. No matter how many more pairs I gets through before I kicks the bucket, there'll never be another pair of magic carpet slippers.'